S0-EDP-697
Columbia Bible College
34444000972034

COUNTING MY FRIENDS

Selma Hooge

Illustrated by
Michael Martchenko

Selma Hooge

DANCING SUN BOOKS, *an imprint of*
gage EDUCATIONAL PUBLISHING COM
A DIVISION OF CANADA PUBLISHING CORP
TORONTO ONTARIO CANADA

To

Sarah, our granddaughter

Copyright © 1993 Gage Educational Publishing Company
A Division of Canada Publishing Corporation

All rights reserved. No part of this work covered by the copyrights
hereon may be reproduced or used in any form or by any means–
graphic, electronic, electrostatic, or mechanical–without the prior
written permission of the publisher or, in case of photocopying or
other reprographic copying, a licence from the Canadian Reprography
Collective.

Any request for photocopying, recording, taping or information
storage and retrieval systems of any part of this book shall be directed
in writing to the Canadian Reprography Collective, 214 King Street
West, Suite 312, Toronto, Ontario, M5N 2S6.

Canadian Cataloguing in Publication Data

Hooge, Selma
    Counting my friends

ISBN 0-7715-**6959-9**

1. Counting - Juvenile literature. I. Martchenko, Michael. II Title.
QA113.H66 1992 j513.2'11 C92-094615-1

Designer: Pronk&Associates

Illustrator: Michael Martchenko

ISBN 0-7715-**6959-9**

1 2 3 4 5 KW 96 95 94 93 92

Printed in Singapore

No friends, I am alone.

Please call me on the phone.

COLUMBIA BIBLE COLLEGE

5

One friend and I make two.

Our bikes are green and blue.

Two friends
and I
make three.

We run
and climb a tree.

Three friends and I
make four.

10

COLUMBIA BIBLE COLLEGE

We want to eat some more.

Four friends and I make five.

Someday we'll learn to drive.

Five friends and I make six.

Our dogs can do great tricks.

Six friends and I make seven.

We build a cart for Kevin.

Seven friends and I make eight.

We run to hide and wait.

Eight friends and I make nine.

We march in one straight line.

Nine friends and I make ten.

Time to go home again!